BR WOLVERINE
Macri, Thomas
This is Wolverine /

031215

THIS IS WOLVERINE

By Thomas Macri

Illustrated by Carlo Barberi *and* Hi-Fi Design

Based on the Marvel comic book series Wolverine

ABDO
Spotlight

MARVEL
New York

WWW.ABDOPUBLISHING.COM

Reinforced library bound edition published in 2015 by Spotlight, a division of ABDO
PO Box 398166, Minneapolis, Minnesota 55439. Spotlight produces high-quality
reinforced library bound editions for schools and libraries. Published by Marvel Press,
an imprint of Disney Book Group.

Printed in the United States of America, North Mankato, Minnesota.
052014
072014

marvelkids.com

© 2013 MARVEL

THIS BOOK CONTAINS
RECYCLED MATERIALS

CATALOGING-IN-PUBLICATION DATA

Macri, Thomas.
This is Wolverine / by Thomas Macri ; illustrated by Carlo Barberi and Hi-Fi Design.
   p. cm. -- (World of reading. Level 1)
Summary: Meet and learn all about Wolverine.
1. Wolverine (Fictitious characters)--Juvenile fiction. 2. Superheroes--Juvenile fiction. I.
Barberi, Carlo, ill. II. Hi-Fi Colour Design, ill. III. Title. IV. Series.
[Fic]--dc23

978-1-61479-256-7   (Reinforced Library Bound Edition)

Spotlight

A Division of ABDO
www.abdopublishing.com

This is Wolverine.

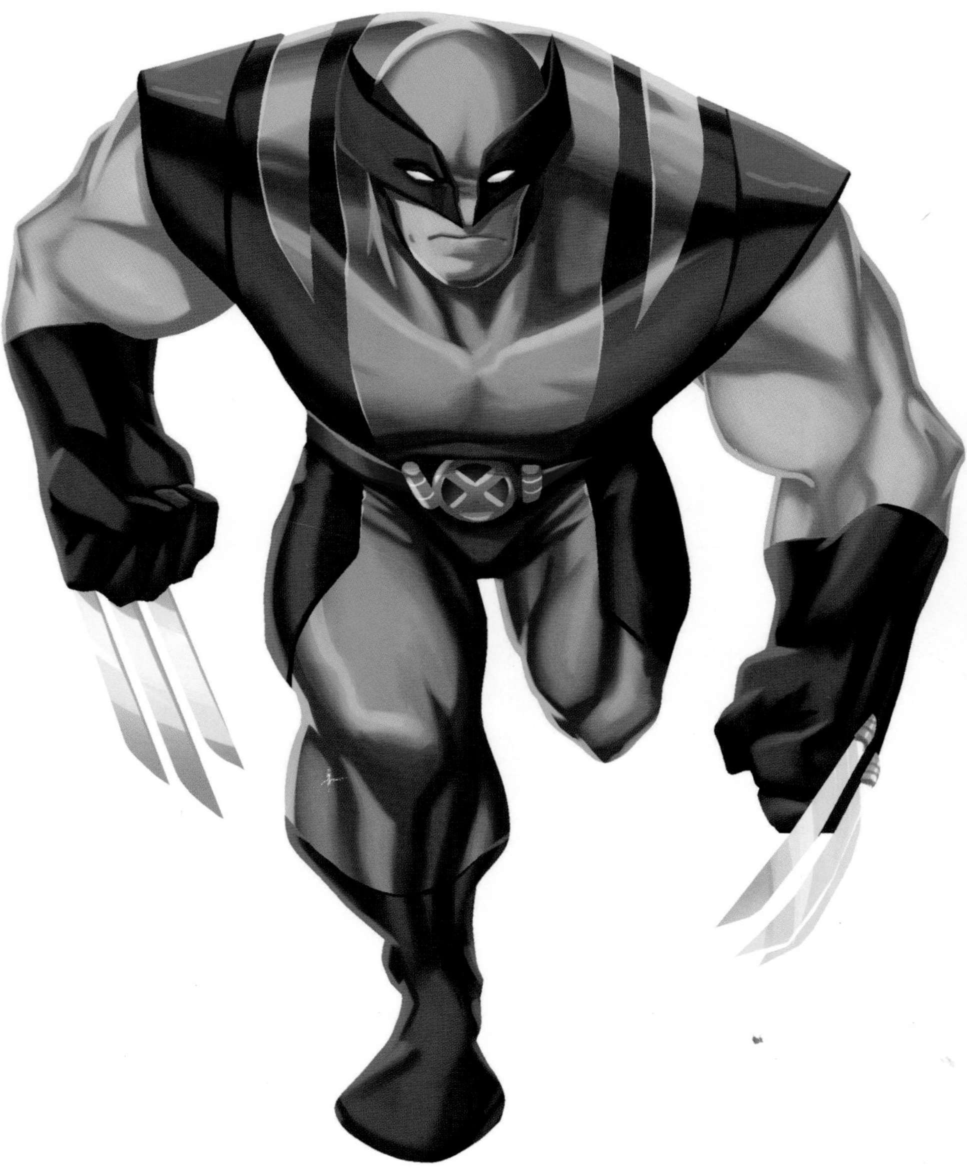

He is a Super Hero.
He fights bad guys.

He is a mutant.
He was born with powers.

He has claws.
They are sharp!

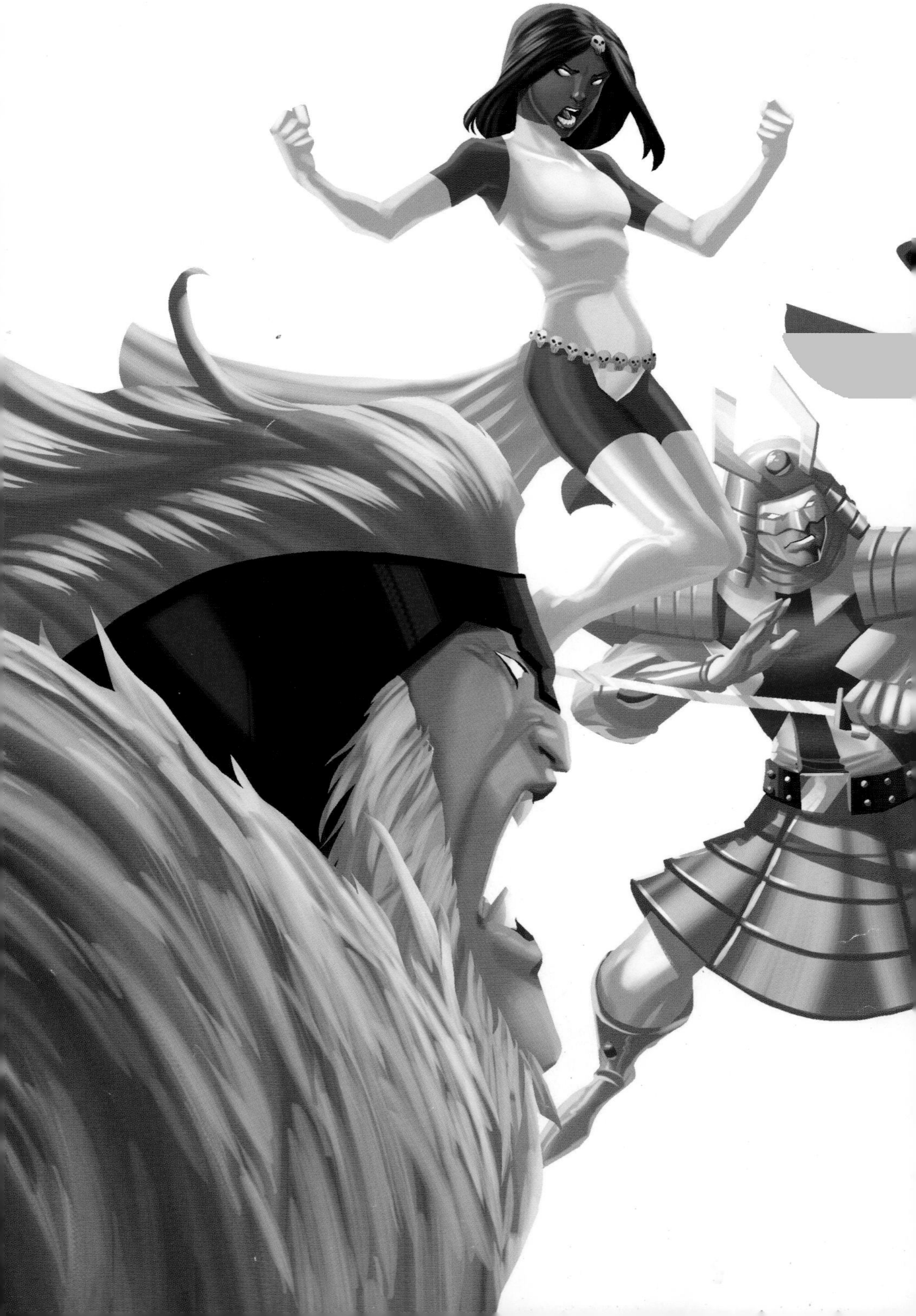

Sometimes he fights
alone.

Sometimes he is part
of a team.

They are called
The X-Men.

Wolverine wears a
mask.
He wears a costume.

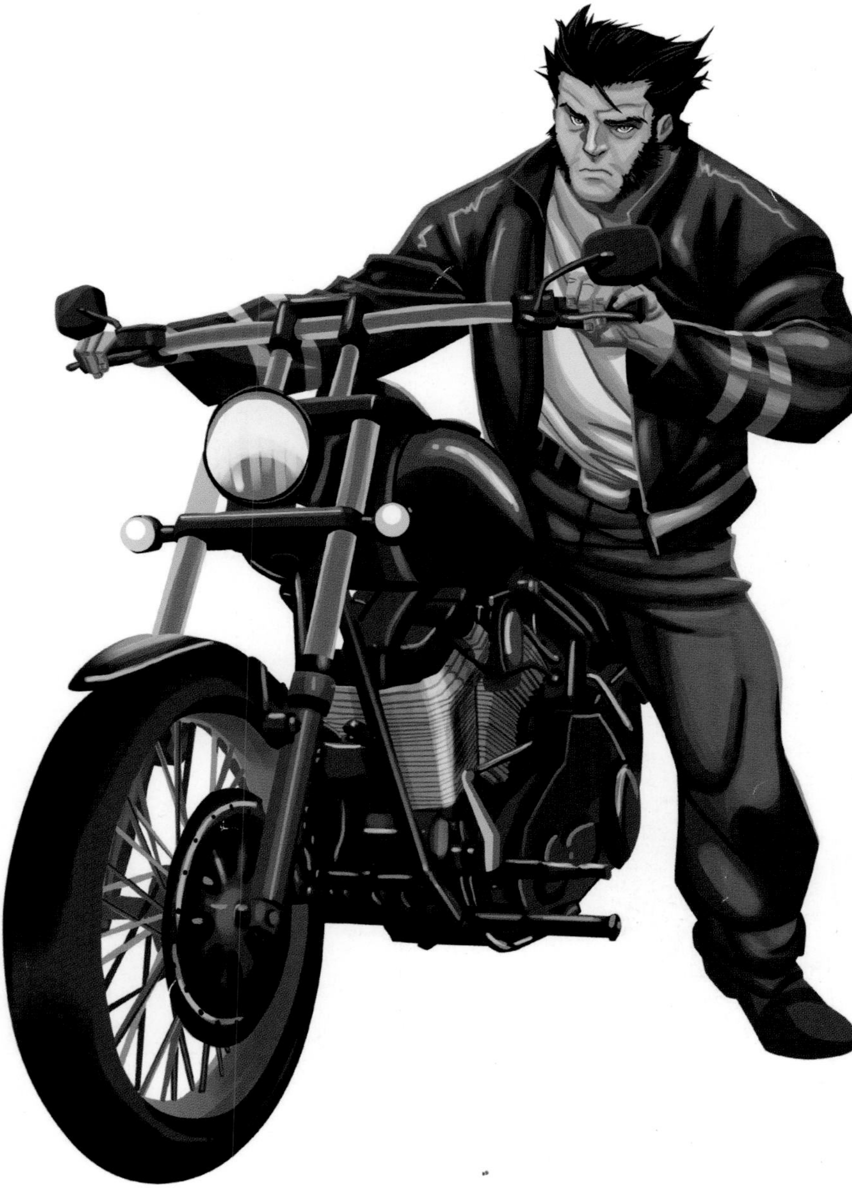

His real name is Logan.

His job is dangerous.

He gets hurt.

He heals quickly.

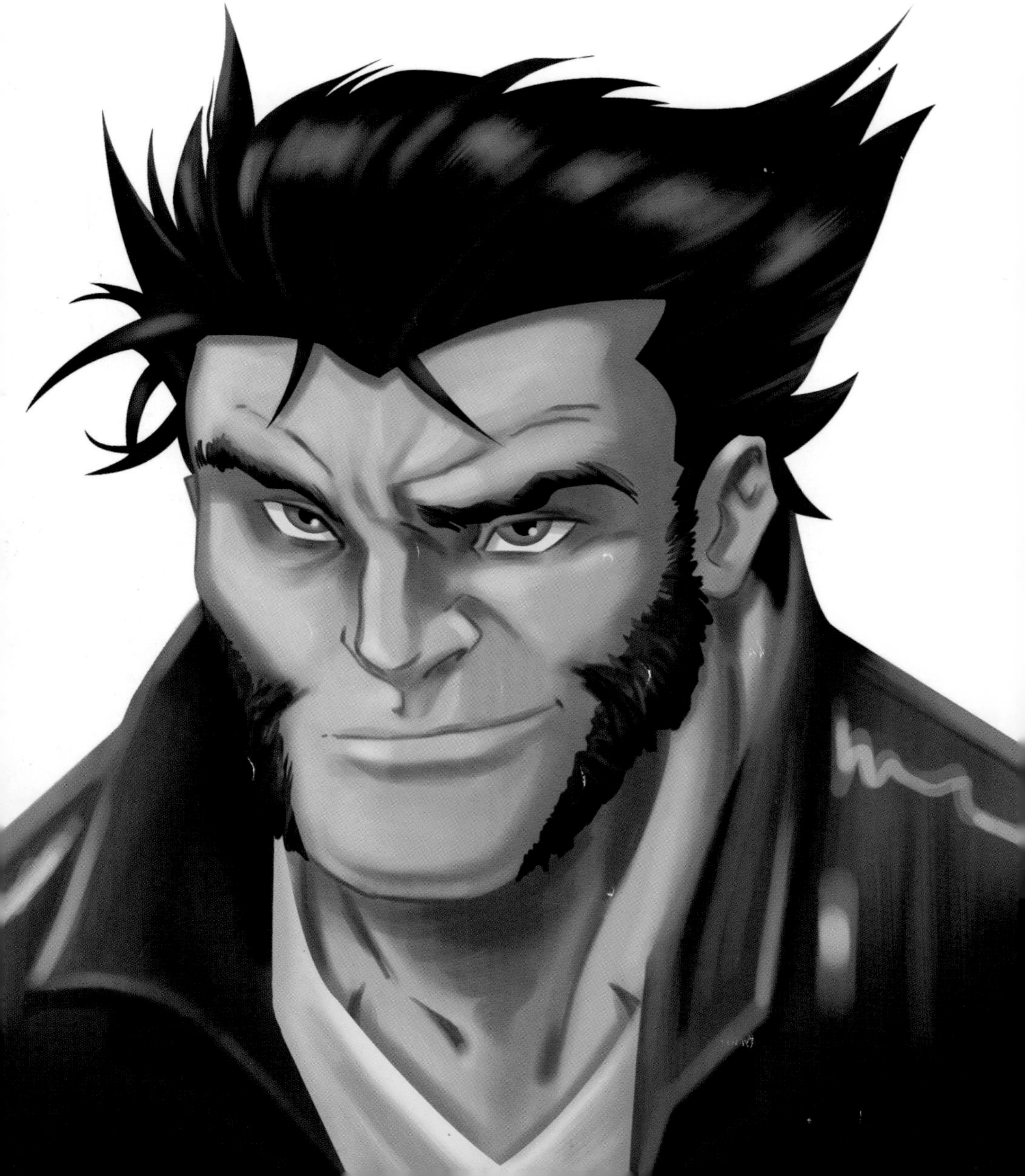

He is strong.
His bones are strong.
His claws are strong.

Nothing can break them.
Not even the Hulk.

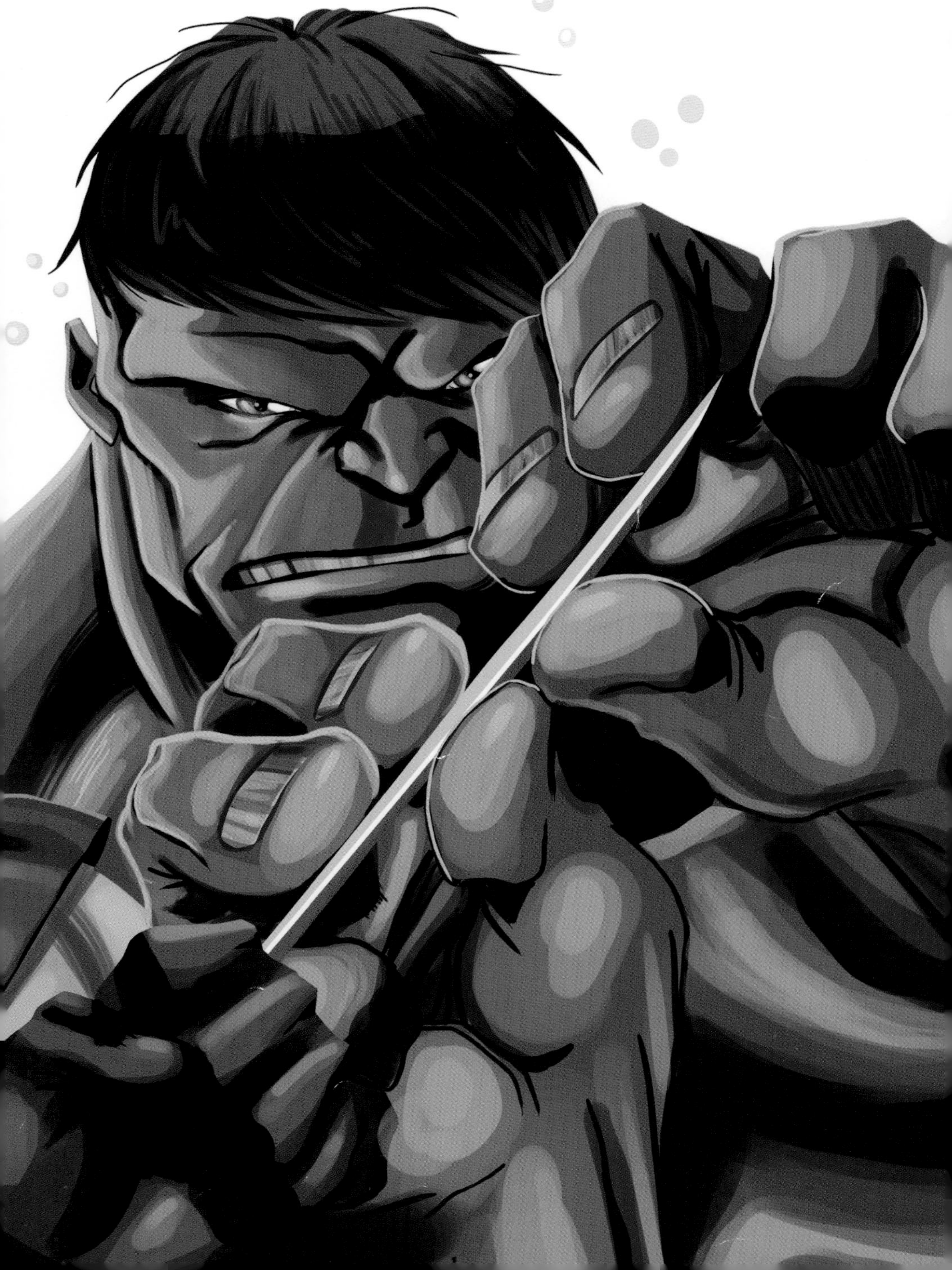

Wolverine has great
senses.
He can smell like a wolf.

He can hear like a bat.

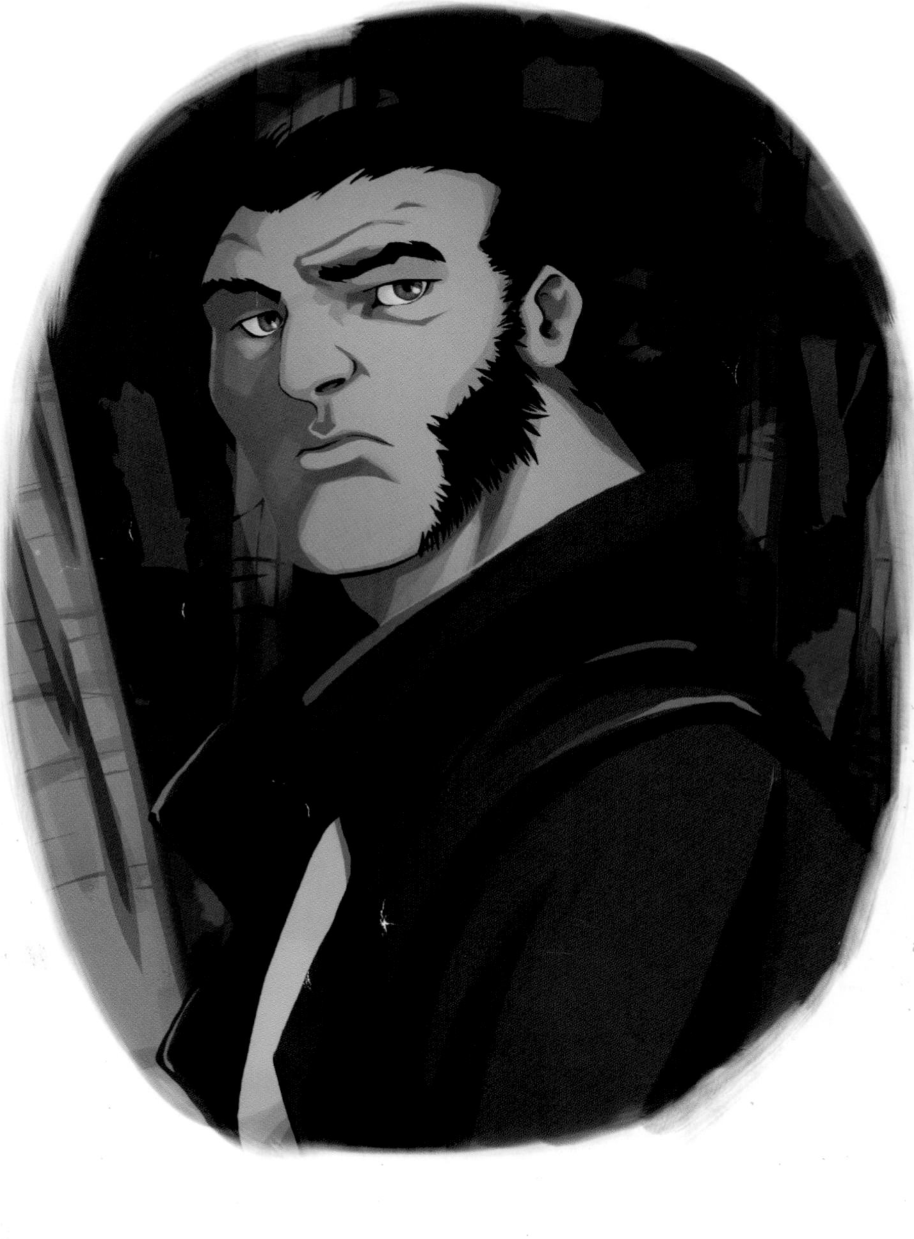

He senses danger.

He puts on his costume.

He runs as fast as
a hound.

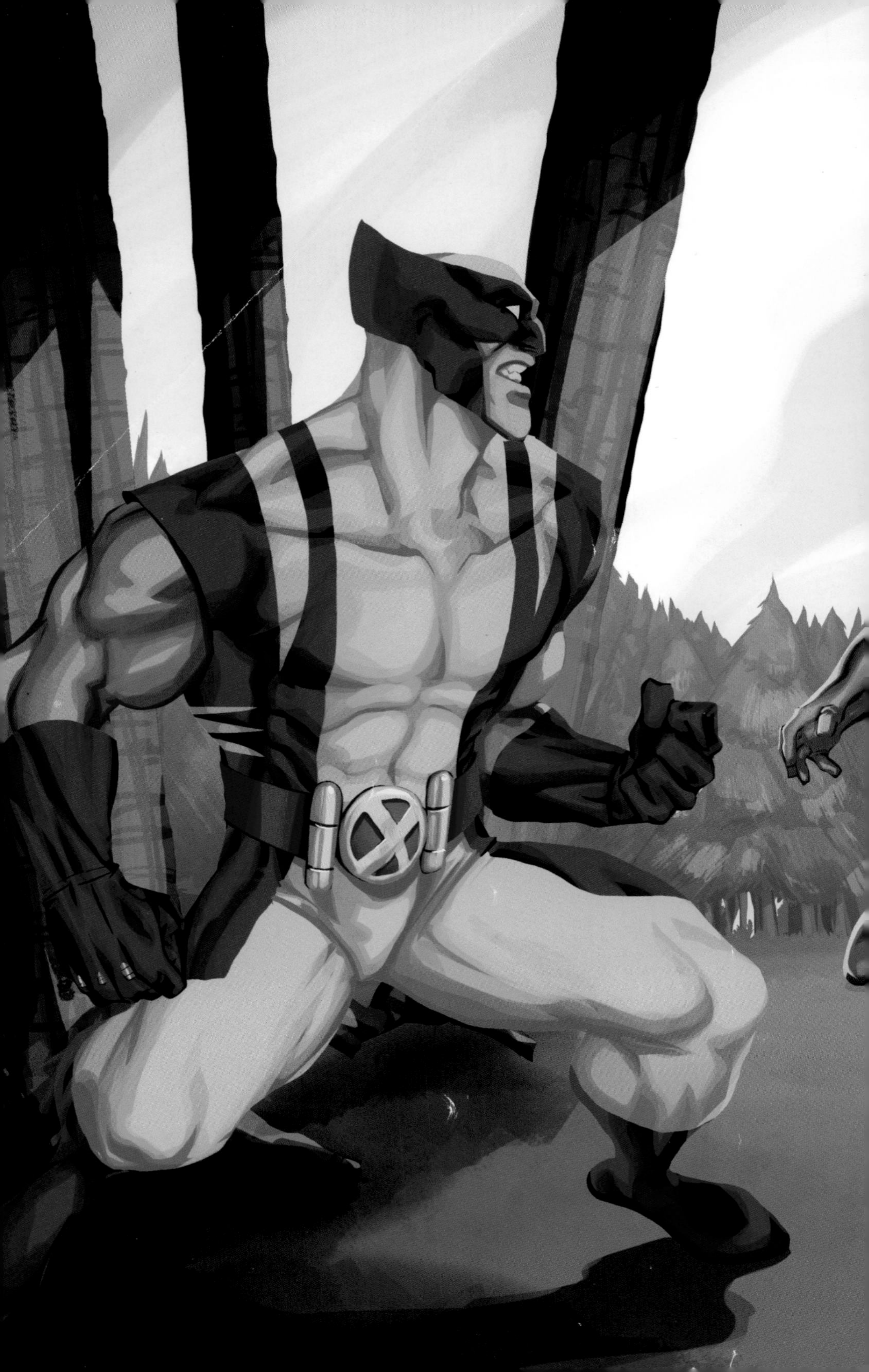

He sees the X-Men.
They are in danger.

Wolverine attacks!

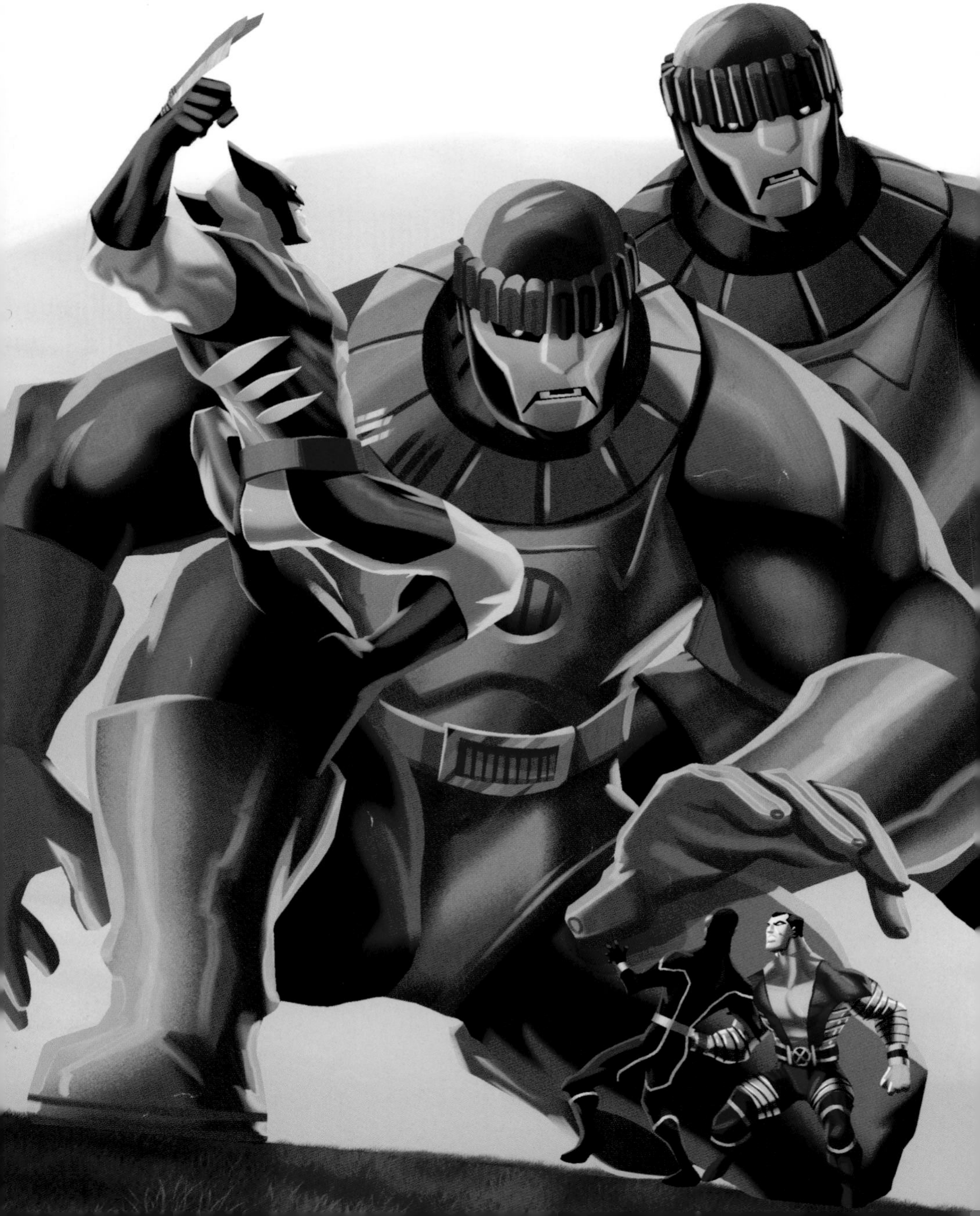

His claws cut metal.

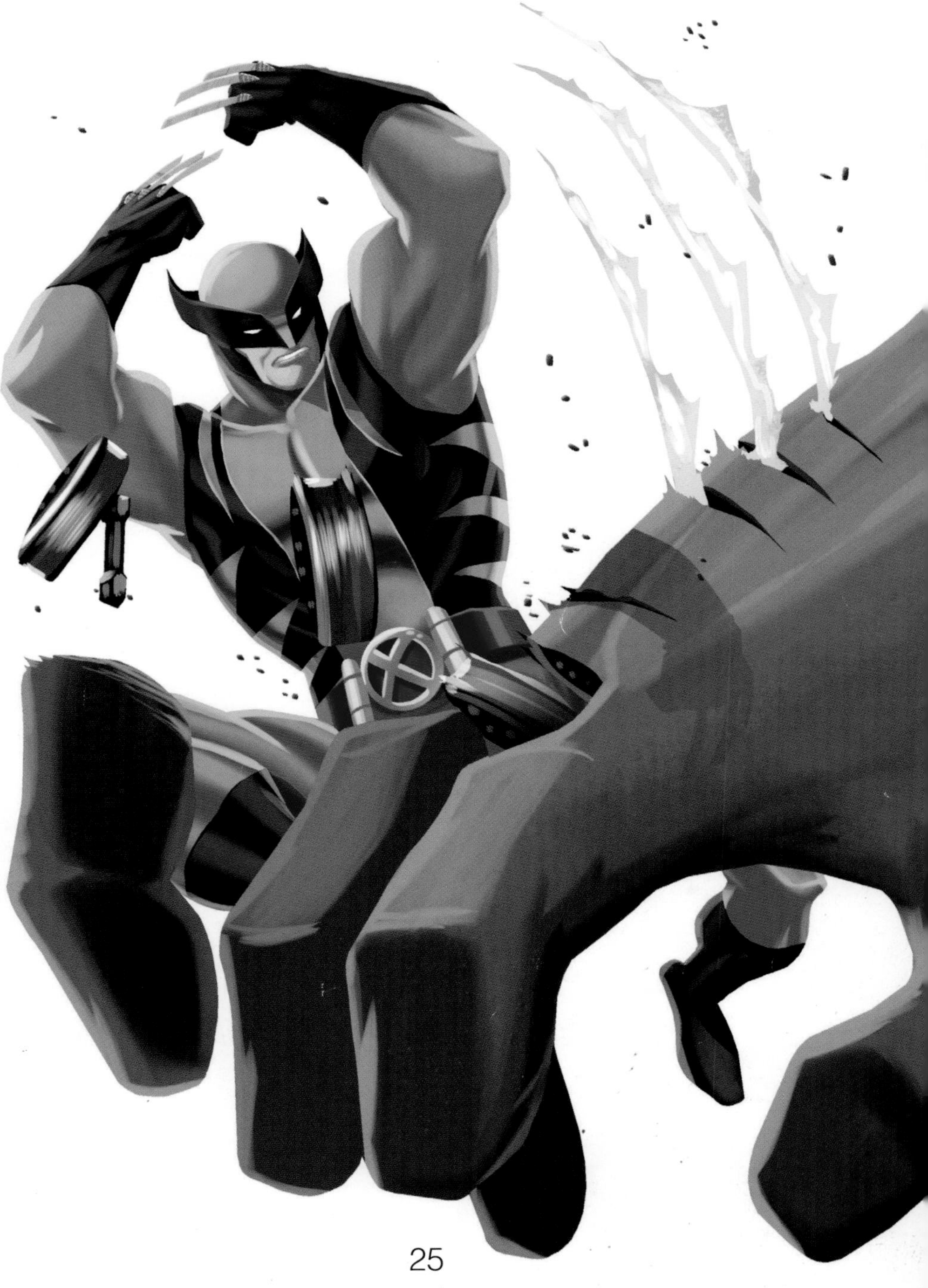

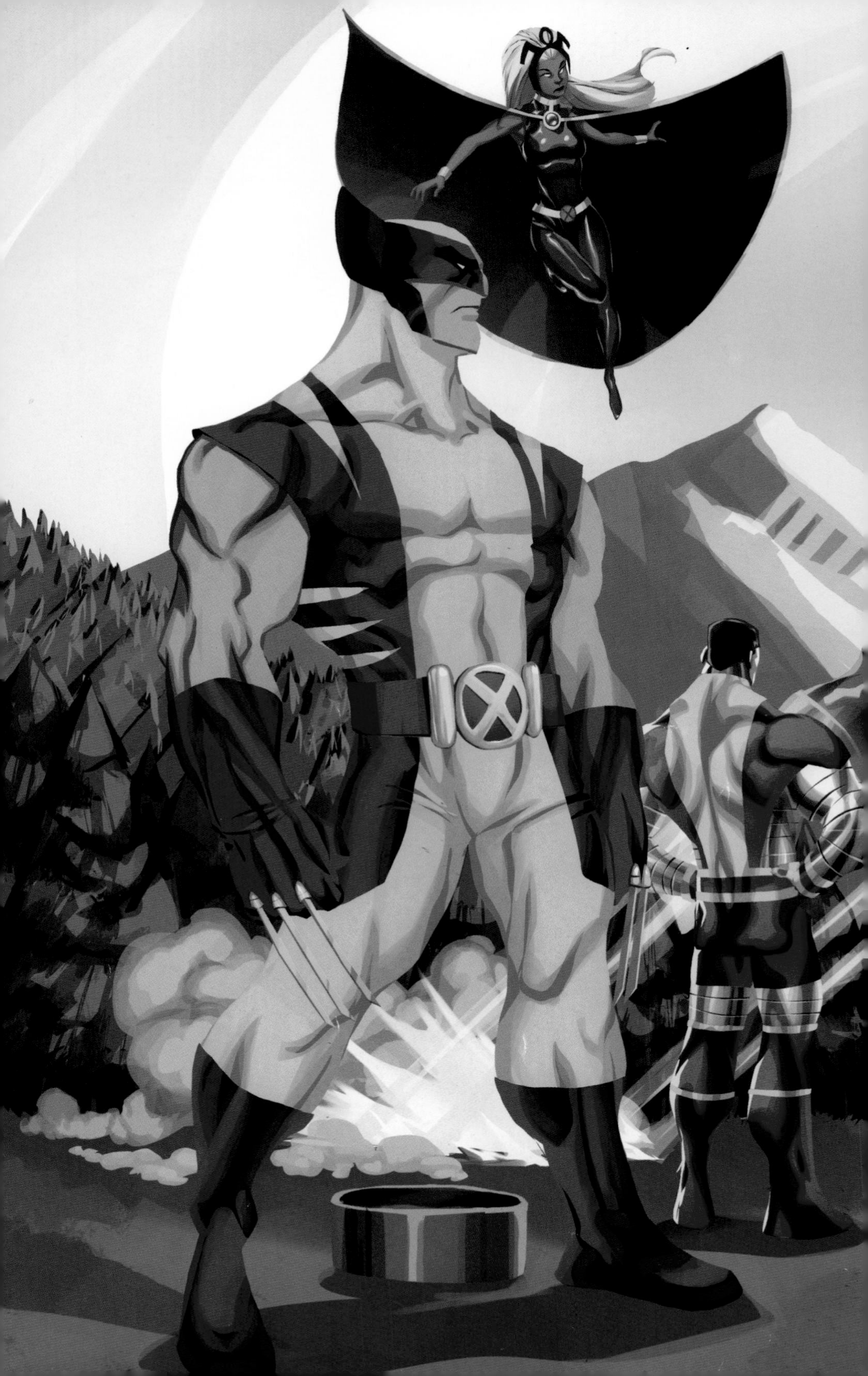

He saves his friends!

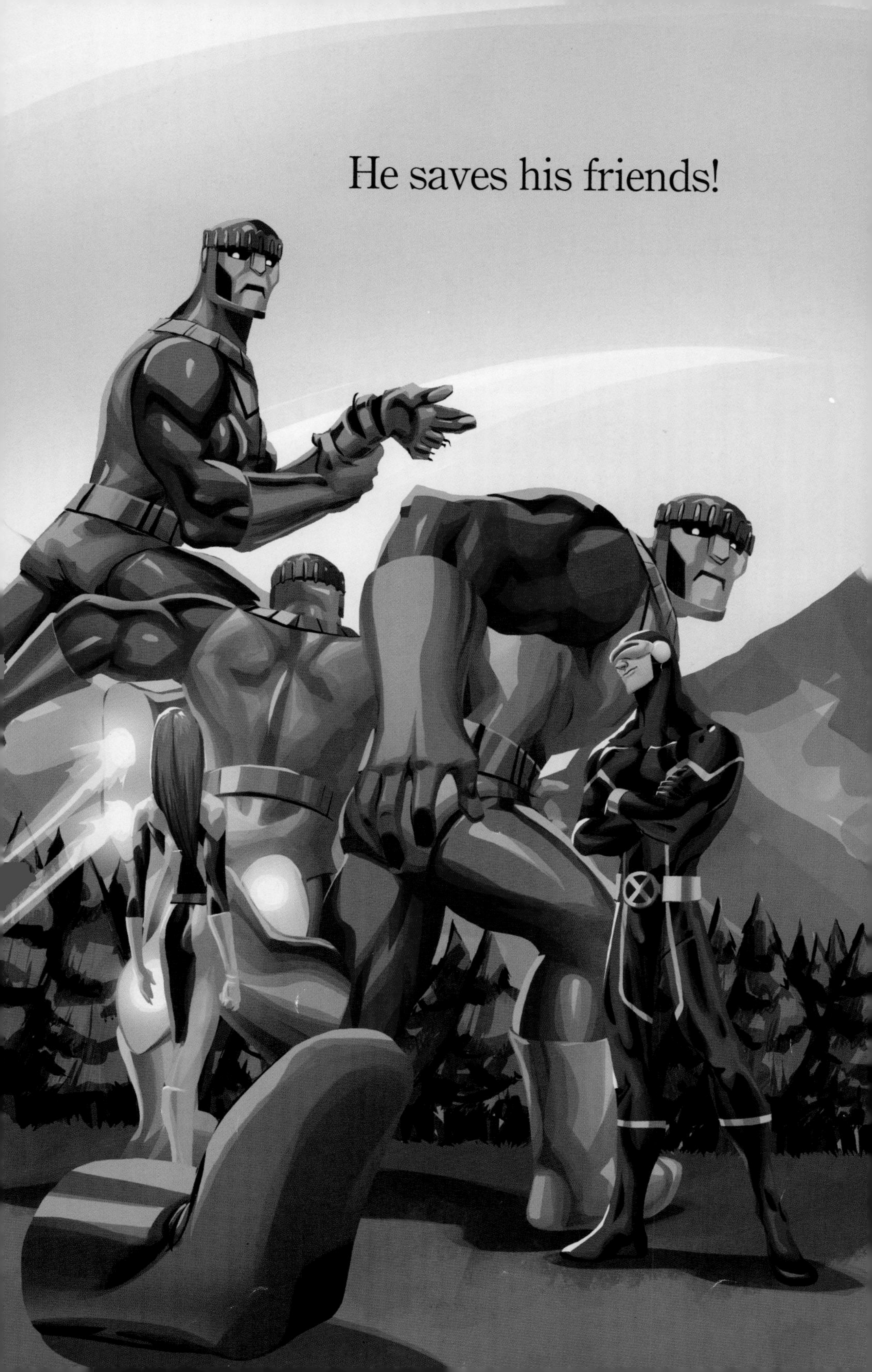

Sometimes he works with
The X-Men.

Sometimes he
works alone.

But he always does
a good job.

He is a mutant.
He is a Super Hero.

He is Wolverine.

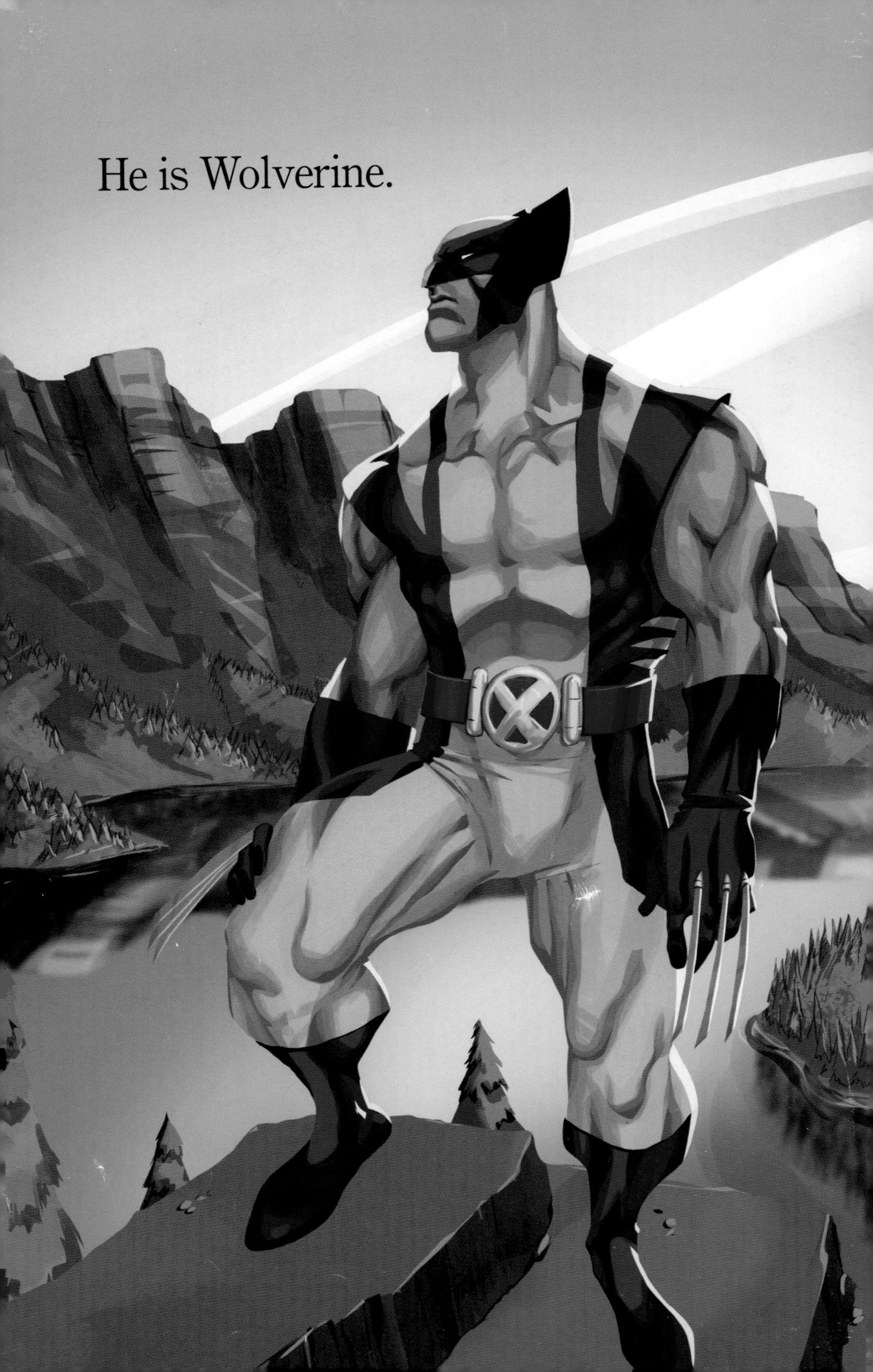